D1371439

OUR AMAZING WORLD

NATURAL 1

TECTUM
junior

OTTAWA PUBLIC LIBRARY
BIBLIOTHEQUE PUBLIQUE D'OTTAWA

Tectum Junior

© 2011 Tectum Publishers NV
Godefriduskaai 22
2000 Antwerp
Belgium
p. +32 3 226 66 73
f. +32 3 226 53 65
info@tectum.be
www.tectum.be

ISBN: 978-9079761-04-3
WD: 2011/9021/73
(J005 US)

EDITED AND DESIGNED by PICOpublications Milano
www.picopublications.com
DESIGN AND LAYOUT © PICOpublications Milano 2011
TEXT © PICOpublications Milano 2011
EDITOR Mariarosaria Tagliaferri
SCIENTIFIC ADVISOR Francesco Tomasinelli
TEXTS Mariarosaria Tagliaferri
SCIENTIFIC ADVISOR Francesco Tommasinelli
ILLUSTRATION Chiara Buccheri, Chiara Ricci (Galapagos Island, Grand Canyon National Park)
LAYOUT Chiara Borda
TYPESETTING Maurizio Grassi
COVER Chiara Buccheri, Mariarosaria Tagliaferri, Chiara Ricci
ENGLISH TRANSLATION Cillero & De Motta, Cheryl Whittaker

No part of this book may be reproduced in any form,
By print, photo print, microfilm or any other means
Without written permission from the publisher.

All facts in this book have been researched with utmost precision.
However we can neither be held responsible for any inaccuracies
nor for subsequent loss or damage arising therefrom.

Unless otherwise noted all product images are used by courtesy
of the respective companies mentioned in the product description.

Printed in China

WHAT ARE THE SITES CHOSEN BY UNESCO TO BE LISTED AS WORLD HERITAGE?

n order to encourage international cooperation in the conservation of our world's cultural and natural heritage, **UNESCO** has issued a list of sites that are of outstanding value to the history of our planet and he evolution of human civilization. No matter how remote, or what their age, they belong to all human beings, and most of all to children. In these pages you will discover **breathtaking waterfalls**, **the secrets of the giant panda**, and **truly unique animals on the Galapagos Islands**, as well as many of the other treasures of our world. Choose your favorite sites and help to protect their irreplaceable value.

SWEDEN
24 Laponian Area

ROMANIA
22 Danube Delta

CHINA
14 Sichuan
Giant Panda
Sanctuaries Wolong,
Mt Siguninan
and Jiajin Mountains

USA
6 Grand
Canyon

ITALY
18 Aeolian
Islands

INDIA
16 Kaziranga
National Park

ECUADOR
4 Galapagos
Islands

TURKEY
28 Hierapolis
Pamukkale

TANZANIA
26 Kilimanjaro
National Park

BRAZIL
12 Central Amazon
Conservation complex

ARGENTINA
8 Peninsula Valdés

MALAWI
20 Lake Malawi

AUSTRALIA
10 Uluru-Kata Tjuta
National Park

ZIMBABWE-ZAMBIA
30 Victoria Falls

If you put all the zoos and aquariums in the world together, the result still wouldn't compare with the inhabitants of this archipelago of 19 islands. The nearest coastline is over 620 miles away, so the animals have been able to live in absolute peace for centuries without outside interference or human contact. The only people to visit from time to time were pirates. Its remote location has kept the same environment for thousands of years. Even today, it isn't easy to get to the Galapagos. First, you have to go to Quito, the capital of Ecuador. You have to take another flight from there to the Galapagos and then a boat if you want to travel from one island to another. Try to imagine how difficult that wa[s] 200 years ago! Nearly 200 years ago, on December 2[7], 1831, a British exploration ship, the *Beagle* (like the dog), lef[t] England, reaching the Galapagos on September 15, 1835 a voyage of nearly four years! On board was Charles Darwi[n] a young student who was keen on animals and nature.

For some time, a theory based on the evolution o[f] species had been going around in his mind. He becam[e] convinced of his theory in the Galapagos.

Here is a marine iguana. It is the only lizard that lives by the sea and cannot survive without it. It feeds on the seaweed it finds on the seabed and can stay underwater for over an hour. When they are on land, these creatures spend most of the time sunning themselves on the rocks in large colonies. They are only found in the Galapagos.

WHAT DID DARWIN SEE THAT WAS SO AMAZING?

First of all, he observed the *Phalacrocorax harrisi*, a flightless cormorant. What? Birds that don't fly? That's right. But they are excellent swimmers and, if you think about it, they survive by eating mainly fish. Darwin then noticed the presence of *Geochelone elephantopus* in large numbers. These were large tortoises over five feet in length that ate cactus, leaves and lichen. He also saw *Conolophus subcristatus*, an iguana that seems to have come right out of Jurassic Park. Darwin also observed other strange birds, like the *Sula nebouxii*. This bird seems to be wearing blue socks, so it comes as no surprise that it is also known as the 'Blue-footed Booby'!

ORIGIN OF THE SPECIES

When Darwin returned to England, he wrote a very successful book, which is still the basis of numerous scientific studies today. His travels, particularly in the Galapagos, allowed him to discover a lot of important information.

The special conditions found on these islands and the opportunity he was given to see how evolution worked were inspirational. Would you like to know how it works?

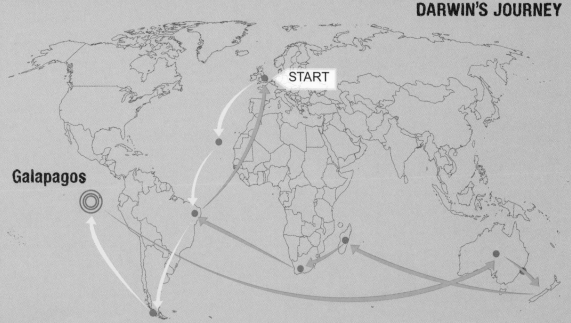

START

Galapagos

IT'S TIME FOR AN EXPERIMENT

Take two seeds from the same plant and plant one of them at home and the other in a place far away from you and outside (your grandparents' or a friend's home, and even better if it's by the sea or in the country). Treat them the same and give them the same amount of water. In a few weeks, they will have grown. They will be the same, but also different.

The light, type of water, pollution, pollen and insects affect the plants' development. Their growth depends on environmental conditions. Clearly, depending on the complexity of animals and plants, the way they develop is different. Your seedlings will be like Darwin's tortoises, which were different depending on which island they were found on.

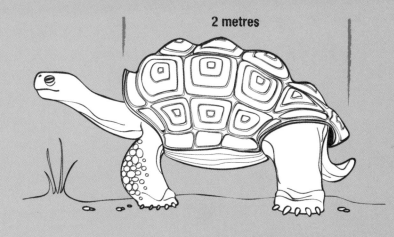

2 metres

THE GIANT GALAPAGOS TORTOISE

THIS IS THE WORLD'S LARGEST SPECIES OF TORTOISE, MEASURING SIX FEET IN LENGTH AND WEIGHING MORE THAN 660 LBS! IT EATS CLOSE TO 500 DIFFERENT TYPES OF PLANTS AND CAN GO A LONG TIME WITHOUT DRINKING. IT CAN LIVE TO 150 YEARS OF AGE, AND LONGER THAN 250 YEARS IF KEPT IN CAPTIVITY. THERE ARE DIFFERENT SUB-SPECIES ON EACH ISLAND.

HOW ARE THINGS IN THE GALAPAGOS NOW?

UNESCO placed the Galapagos site on its World Heritage in Danger list in 2007. Fortunately, the Darwin Foundation has everything under control. Would you like to help out, too? Visit the www.galapagos.org website and you will find out how. Though it seems difficult to believe, the biggest threat comes from other animals, not the local ones but the ones introduced by man. They are ruining the environment and plants and endangering the tortoises, iguanas and birds.

Did you know that the Galapagos Islands are home to the only species of tropical penguins, the ones that live the furthest north of all?
Quiz: where do the other penguins live?

(solution on page 32)

GRAND CANYON

If the Earth were a cake, the Grand Canyon would be a slice showing us the ingredients and layers.

The planet's entire history can be read from the bottom to the top if you are standing in this deep rift. Unique in the world because of its size, the Grand Canyon is also a microcosm of all the habitats to be found in North America, from Mexico to Canada.

The different environments, from alpine to desert, influence the climate. Temperatures vary between 1.4 and 98.6° F.

This area was once home to the PUEBLO Indians who dug their houses into the rock.

As a result of 'orogeny' occurring about 65 MILLION YEARS AGO, part of the land was raised to form the COLORADO PLATEAU.

OROGENY

The process leading to the formation of mountains. Sideways movements originating from forces at the center of the Earth cause the different layers to become stacked.

If the Plateau can be explained as the result of orogeny, then how was the Canyon created? It's the result of constant erosion by water since the Cenozoic Era.

GEOLOGICAL ERAS THAT CAN BE 'READ' IN THE GRAND CANYON

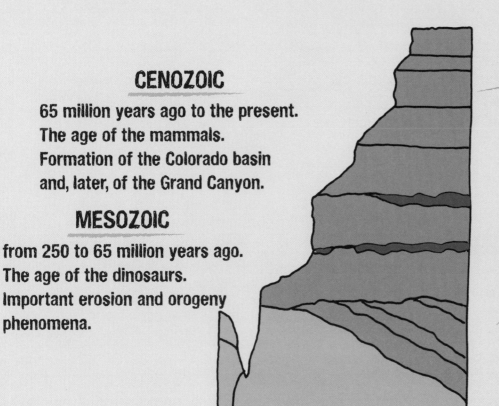

CENOZOIC

65 million years ago to the present.
The age of the mammals.
Formation of the Colorado basin
and, later, of the Grand Canyon.

MESOZOIC

from 250 to 65 million years ago.
The age of the dinosaurs.
Important erosion and orogeny
phenomena.

PALEOZOIC

from 540 to 250 million years ago.
Beginnings of many present-day
animals and plants such as ferns,
conifers, reptiles, amphibians, fish
and insects.

PRECAMBRIAN

from approximately
4 billion to 540 million
years ago.

BY OBSERVING THE CANYON WALLS AN INCH AT A TIME, RESEARCHERS
HAVE FOUND THE FOSSILS OF DIFFERENT PRIMITIVE LIFE FORMS.
PLANTS, SMALL ANIMALS AND FISH CONFIRM THE PRESENCE OF WATER
FROM THE RIVER, BUT ALSO FROM THE PACIFIC OCEAN.

THE MOST COMMON ANIMALS FOUND
ALONG THE COLORADO RIVER INCLUDE
REPTILES AND BIRDS, IN ADDITION TO
RODENTS AND BATS. ANOTHER ANIMAL
FOUND THERE THAT, ALTHOUGH NOT VERY
BEAUTIFUL, IS CERTAINLY AWE-INSPIRING,
IS THE BALD-HEADED CALIFORNIA CONDOR.

THE CALIFORNIA CONDOR

Is a species of vulture and is the largest bird in North
America, with a wingspan of almost 10 feet! This rare bird
has been at the center of a large and expensive, but highly
successful, conservation project.

**WHERE DOES THE GRAND
CANYON END?**
It ends at a waterfall that
feeds into Lake Mead, which
is located in the states
of Nevada and Arizona.

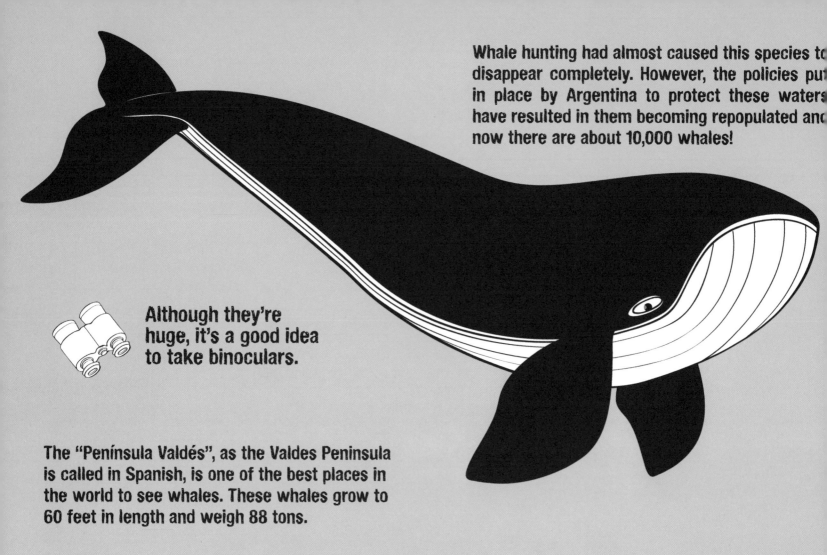

Whale hunting had almost caused this species to disappear completely. However, the policies put in place by Argentina to protect these waters have resulted in them becoming repopulated and now there are about 10,000 whales!

Although they're huge, it's a good idea to take binoculars.

The "Península Valdés", as the Valdes Peninsula is called in Spanish, is one of the best places in the world to see whales. These whales grow to 60 feet in length and weigh 88 tons.

They come here to reproduce and it isn't unusual to see mothers and their infants. You can board a small boat in Puerto Pirámides to see these wonderful creatures close up. These whales can actually also be seen from the coast because they stay on the surface to feed on plankton, small crustaceans and fish. The best time to see them is in November and December.

Spheniscus magellanicus is the scientific name for the Magellan penguin that lives in this area. It is close to two and a half feet tall and weighs between 6.5 and 11 lbs. Magellan penguins form gigantic colonies when it's time to reproduce. A little distance from the Valdes Peninsula, in Punta Tombo, there are half a million penguins in only three-quarters of a square mile! The males arrive on land first to build nests in the ground or among the bushes. The females arrive a few weeks later. After a period of courtship, they reproduce. After 40 days of being kept warm and safe from predators, the eggs hatch. The newly-hatched penguins are barely five inches long and weigh little more than one and a half ounces!

In the Chubut region of northern Patagonia is one of the world's largest nature reserves for marine fauna: the Valdes Peninsula. Its squat shape protects the coastal waters of two gulfs, the Golfo Nuevo to the south and Golfo San José to the north. The wildlife found on land includes rheas, maras (large and unusual rodents), guanacos and even hairy armadillos. Its beaches are home to sea lions, elephant seals and penguins. Its waters are the realm of whales and orcas, while the sky is filled with hundreds of bird species, many of which are migratory birds. What are they all doing here? These beaches, quiet inlets and seas are places where these animals can live undisturbed!

It is also one of the few places on the planet where marine mammals can reproduce instead of becoming extinct. It also helps that it benefits from the currents reaching it from the Central Atlantic and the Falkland Islands, which are rich in nutrients and plankton. There's plenty of food available 24 hours a day!

Sea lions eat between 33 and 55 lbs of fish, octopus and squid each day. But sometimes they are the ones that are eaten!

Not everybody likes plankton – or hunters on the beach. The orca or killer whale is a carnivore that manages to swim up to the beach, where it catches young elephant seals and sea lions. It has an amazing technique. It hides in the waves and seizes animals on the shore with an extraordinary twisting action. Then it takes advantage of the waves again to return to the water.

HERE IS WHERE THE WORLD'S LARGEST SEAL LIVES

This place is also the home of the world's largest seal – the southern elephant seal. Adult males of this species can grow to nearly 20 feet in length and weigh 4 tons. They can dive to a depth of 3,281 feet and stay underwater for more than an hour to catch mollusks. Their name comes from their long snout, which resembles a trunk.

3 feet

20 feet

AUSTRALIA
THE ULURU-KATA TJUTA NATIONAL PARK

The Uluru-Kata Tjuta National Park lies in the heart of Australia in an arid, almost desert-like region where it rains little and the temperatures can be extreme.

It's world famous because of Ayers Rock, the most famous Australian natural landmark: a large rock formation that rises from the red earth.

This is the Australian Outback, a semi-desert area that is the most remote part of the continent, but also one of the most interesting habitats in the country.

A great many plants and animals are to be found here that are not found anywhere else in the world, such as wallabies and the giant goanna.

This is also the land where some of the oldest groups of humans in the world live: the Aborigines.

With the appearance of a giant loaf of bread, this rock measures 5.8 miles in diameter at its widest point and rises 1,115 feet above the surrounding plain.

The incredible color of AYERS ROCK is due to the elevated iron content in the rock, which has been oxidizing (a process of surface chemical alteration caused by the oxygen-rich air) over thousands of years.

THE BLACK-HEADED PYTHON OR WOMA

This is one of the most beautiful constrictor snakes (pythons and boas) in the world. Measuring six and a half feet in length, it is beige with darker brown stripes. It is a protected species today and is one of the species symbolizing the park. It eats small marsupials, reptiles and birds.

MOLOCH

This is another amazing animal and icon of the Australian Outback. This lizard is completely covered in spines and measures some eight inches in length. With its fearsome appearance, the thorny devil, as it is also known, is completely harmless. It only eats ants and it drinks by licking water droplets that form on its body and between its spines in the early morning.

The secret of Ayers Rock

This rock is 500 million years old (made of sandstone, a sedimentary rock) and is the visible part of an ancient rock layer that has re-emerged from the desert soil.

ULURU

Europeans discovered this rock only 800 years ago, but for the Aborigines, known as Anangu, it is called 'Uluru', which means 'island mountain'.

Nineteen miles from Uluru are the Kata Kata Mountains. This name literally means 'many heads'.

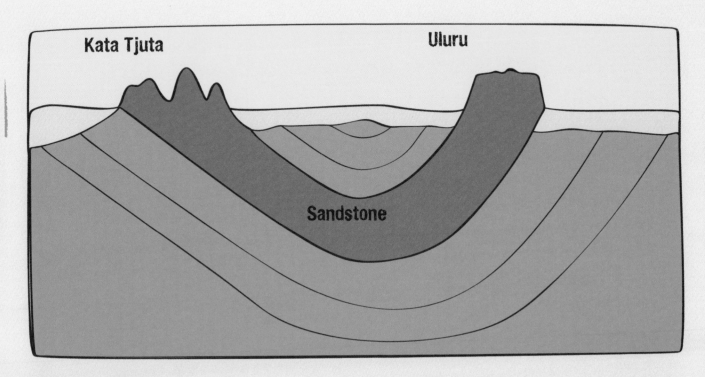

Kata Tjuta   Uluru

Sandstone

FOR THE ANANGU, this place is closely associated with the idea of the 'Dreamtime', a remote period of time, and to the Tjukurita, ancestral beings with human or animal attributes from whom the Anangu received their code of behavior and on which their social order is based.

What animal species do these belong to: the great desert skink, the mulga and the goanna?

You all know what a kangaroo looks like; but do you know the difference between a kangaroo and a wallaby?

And between a bilby and a bettong?

(Answers on page 32)

CENTRAL AMAZON CONSERVATION COMPLEX

Hidden in the heart of Brazil, this is South America's largest forest reserve, with an area of more than 5 million hectares. To give you an idea of its size, it's bigger than Switzerland. When people speak of tropical rainforests and jungles, they immediately think of the Amazon Rainforest. The Conservation Complex is a special part of the Amazon Rainforest, consisting of lowland forests that are seasonally flooded by the River Amazon and its tributaries.

At the beginning of each year, when it rains the most, a large part of the forest is submerged under many feet of water, giving rise to an ecosystem on a scale that is unequalled on any other continent. During the flood season, there are many unusual scenes, such as fish swimming amongst the trees or small and large plant islands tha move on the currents created in the floodwaters.

Everything changes so quickly that there are no reliable maps of the area. The humidity, heat, fruit, leaves and organic material carried by the water all favor the development of unique biodiversity – reptiles, amphibians, fish and some truly special mammals. There are fish that have evolved in relation to species of trees that produce fleshy fruit. When the water rises, the fish can reach the fruit.

The Tambaqui (*Collosoma macropamum*) specializes in eating the fruit of the *Hevea spruceana* tree.

The water rises more than 30 feet!

THE RIVER DOLPHIN ("INIA GEOFFRENSIS")

Known locally as a *boto*, this is a dolphin that adapted to living in the freshwater of the Amazon and its tributaries millions of years ago. It is a very unique pinkish-gray color and grows to a length of eight feet and a weight of 220 lbs. It can't see very well but has a very sophisticated sonar (even more sensitive than that of its cousins living in the sea), which it uses to find fish in the murky Amazon waters.

Attention: endangered species.

MEANDERS
The river waters advance slowly but relentlessly into the forest and its quiet and constant strength creates sinuous bends among the trees on the plain like giant snakes; these are technically known as 'meanders'.

HOW ARE THESE BENDS FORMED?

The ingredients for this are water and a large plain. Flowing over flat terrain is delicate. The water can go in a straight line until it comes across an obstacle. Sometimes a short and slight slope in the land can cause the course to be diverted and, even more importantly, it can start a process of erosion on one bank and of sediment deposition on the other.

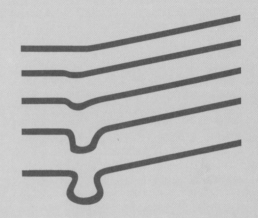

- **4,310 miles** With 4,310 miles, the Amazon is the longest watercourse in the world.

- **5,000 species** Five thousand species of fish live in the river. Many of these fish are extraordinary!

- **16 feet** The arapaima is a giant freshwater fish that can grow up to 16 feet in length. It's the largest river fish in South America.

- **6.5 feet** How about the electric eel? It has the shape of a snake and is six and a half feet long. It produces an electric shock to stun its prey, such as fish and frogs, before swallowing them.

DID YOU KNOW?

One of the Amazon's tributaries is the Rio Negro, which looks like a river made of coffee. From a distance, its waters are almost black. Its color is the result of partially decomposed plant and animal matter in the water.

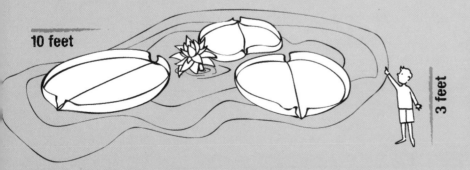

10 feet

3 feet

Is an aquatic plant related to the water lily. It has floating leaves with a diameter of almost 10 feet and can support up to 88 lbs of weight.

SICHUAN GIANT PANDA SANCTUARIES – WOLONG MT SIGUNINAN AND JIAJIN MOUNTAINS

Amongst the snow-capped peaks and misty forested valleys in the heart of the western Chinese region of Sichuan, there are seven nature reserves and new parks that are home to the giant panda, one of the most endangered species of animals in recent years owing to its particular feeding habits.

The 'land of the clouds', as it is known by the Chinese, is not only remarkable for the beauty of its mountains and valleys, depicted by Chinese artists over the ages; nor only for the legends to which this place has given rise. The slopes of these mountains are, in fact, one of the planet's most incredible biodiversity reserves. In a relatively small space, there is a huge variety of plants including alpine, and even tropical, plants! How is this possible? This area alternate mountains that soar to 3.7 miles in altitude, where sma plants grow in the rocks, with lower mountains covered i evergreen forests.

Descending further, there are deciduous trees, unt you reach the valleys where lush ferns and tropical plant grow. This is an impressive variety of flora that include many varieties of bamboo in the zone where the altitude i between 1.1 and 1.9 miles. These alternating expanses are all that remain of the majestic bamboo forests of China which once covered a much larger area. It is bamboo, and the existence of many varieties of this plant, that are key t understanding the struggle for the giant panda's survival.

THE PANDA HAS BECOME TH SYMBOL FOR THE WORLD WILDLIFE FUND (WWF).

"Wo Long" means 'sleeping dragon', because the inhabitan of the valleys thought that the chain of peaks rising along the River Pitiao was actually a dragon that had fallen asleep and turned into mountains.

BIODIVERSITY

What does a big funny bear with eye patches have in common with a tall and flexible plant?

Quite a lot, actually. There are about 1,000 different species of bamboo in nature and they grow to different heights and have different leaves and stems. Some of these plants grow by as much as three feet a day, reaching 130 feet in height, while others grow more slowly and are smaller in size.

But the differences don't end there. Each species has its own way of growing and is susceptible to certain types of disease and insects. If only one species of a plant like bamboo is left, and this species becomes affected by a disease and disappears from the planet, the animals that feed on that plant will soon also disappear.

THE PANDA IS A SPECIAL SPECIES OF BEAR

It should be an omnivore, but, perhaps owing to its legendary laziness, the panda eats bamboo almost exclusively. A panda can spend between 12 and 14 hours a day eating, and when you consider the time it spends searching for the most tender shoots and the time it needs to digest what it eats, it's easy to say that this is an animal that lives to eat. The panda grows to about five feet in height and can weigh between 155 and 350 lbs. It eats as much as 33 lbs of bamboo a day because this food has few calories, and this is why it spends its whole life eating!

PANDAS AREN'T GOOD AT REPRODUCING. THEY DON'T SEE VERY WELL, PLUS THEY'RE LAZY AND ALMOST ALWAYS LIVE ALONE. HOWEVER, WHEN YOU THINK ABOUT IT, THEY'VE BEEN ABLE TO CHANGE A PART OF THEIR BODY IN ORDER TO LIVE BETTER.

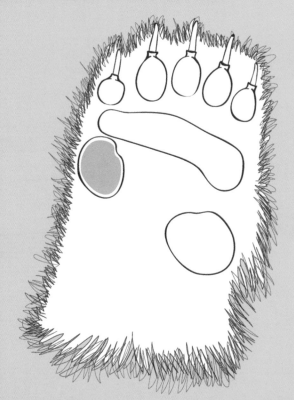 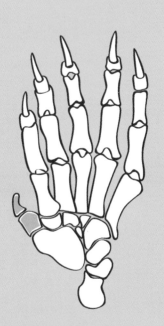 

PANDAS HAVE OPPOSABLE THUMBS, JUST LIKE HUMANS!

In fact, the thumb is the development of a prominent bone that has been modified over time to work like a finger. Life is so much easier with a thumb, especially when you spend so much time eating bamboo!

THE GOLDEN SNUB-NOSED MONKEY

This very beautiful monkey with golden fur and a blue face is confined to the most remote forests.

THE SNOW LEOPARD

This is the undisputed king and symbol of the mountains of Asia. It's very difficult to see one. It lives in the forests and the perennial snow.

HOW IT IS UNIQUE

There are also crocodiles in Kaziranga, but these are very special crocodiles. They are different from all other kinds because they have evolved in harmony with the environment in which they live. One example is the gharial, a crocodile growing to 20 feet in length with a long, narrow snout and small teeth. This weapon works very well in catching its preferred food: it doesn't eat large mammals, only fish.

THE FISHING CAT

Another resident of the park is the fishing cat, a large feline twice the size of a domestic cat. It has learnt to swim well and has a fast and effective style of fishing. It waits on the bank and carefully observes the fish swimming past, before dipping its paw in the water and capturing one. It isn't afraid of humans, but won't let itself be captured easily.

THE KING COBRA

Although it's only 16.5 feet long – half the length of the reticulated python – meeting a king cobra wouldn't be a pleasant experience either. This is the largest venomous snake in the world.

Luckily, it only attacks humans if it is disturbed. It has excellent sight. It has a special organ at the top of its mouth that receives the scent of prey and it can also sense vibrations from anything moving around it. Its jaw can unlock so that it can swallow very large animals without too much trouble.

3 feet

THE RETICULATED PYTHON

Here is something you won't want to meet when going around Kaziranga Park: the reticulated python. It's the world's longest constrictor snake, meaning that it doesn't poison its prey; instead, it squeezes its prey to death. It can grow to 33 feet in length and weigh 66 lbs (with an empty stomach, that is!).

16

KAZIRANGA NATIONAL PARK

The Kaziranga National Park is located in a far corner of India, on the southern bank of the mighty River Brahmaputra. The river, fed by waters from the imposing mountain range of the Himalayas, often breaks its banks during the season of monsoon rains, flooding the surrounding land with its slimy, nutrient-rich waters. It's no wonder that humans stay away from such a place; but this is a good thing for the animals.

Due to the absence of humans and the generosity of the river, Kaziranga is the park with the highest number of large animals on the Indian subcontinent.

Indian elephants, rhinoceroses, buffaloes, swamp deer and gaur (a large wild bovine native to India), in addition to large carnivores such as tigers, leopards and sloth bears live here. The park is also a huge refuge for aquatic birds, including sea eagles, storks and herons.

The existence of parks has been crucial for the protection of these animals, but the crisis isn't over yet.

THE INDIAN RHINOCEROS

The park is a sanctuary for the Indian rhinoceros, an animal that was on the verge of extinction as a result of having been one of the favorite targets of big game hunters for centuries. Of the close to 3,000 of these rhinos on Earth, two thirds are found in Kaziranga and the immediate vicinity.

The nearby large fertile plains provide an ideal habitat. Unlike African rhinos, the Indian variety has an impressive body – six and a half feet tall at the shoulder and weighing over three tons. It has a relatively small single horn and seems to be covered with large plates. Its young are born without a horn. This starts to grow gradually when it is six years old and once it is fully developed, it reaches a length of 10 inches!

AEOLIAN ISLANDS

Lipari, Vulcano, Salina, Stromboli, Filicudi, Alicudi and Panarea are islands in a volcanic archipelago that rise from the warm waters of the Mediterranean Sea. These seven small islands resemble a necklace with a pendant. Millions of years ago, they were active volcanoes that emerged from the sea after powerful eruptions.

Parts of the islands are covered with evergreen vegetation, and every island has a range of colors that immediately reveals their common volcanic nature. However, there are also great differences between them. Lipari, for instance, is very light in color because it has walls of pumice. Pumice is gray and extremely light. This stone can float if thrown int[o] water because it has millions of gas bubbles trapped insid[e] it. Imagine the hot material coming out of the mouth of th[e] volcano and cooling really quickly, trapping the bubbles [of] gas inside its mineral structure!

Unlike Lipari, Vulcano and Stromboli are black, from th[e] top of the islands to the last grain of sand dipping int[o] the sea, and this is quite striking when you approach eithe[r] of them. Even more surprising is the fact that both ar[e] active volcanoes that give off smoke and erupt, sometime[s] frighteningly!

They are an open book for volcanologists and scholars researching changes in the Earth. That's because deep down, our planet is alive and always in motion!

NOT ONLY ERUPTIONS

For centuries, the active volcanoes of the Aeolian Islands have provided information about the Earth and have helped to reveal many of the secret mechanisms which cause eruptions.

There are many other phenomena that can be observed: at the surface, there are geysers and smoke emissions, while underwater emissions of hot air coming from deeper layers can sometimes form thermal springs where the hot water is rich in minerals.

There are even places where the sea is full of bubbles rising to the surface and the air smells of rotten egg.

WHAT IS A VOLCANO?

Volcanoes are mountains that are clear proof of the existence of a fiery mass in the depths of our planet. Volcanoes tell the story of the planet. If you cut a slice from the side of a volcano, you would see at once that it is built of layers. Some layers may be of ash and waste material, while others may be dark and made up of hardened lava. There can also be alternating layers of lava and ash.

A slice of a volcano helps you understand what happened to the earth over millions of years.

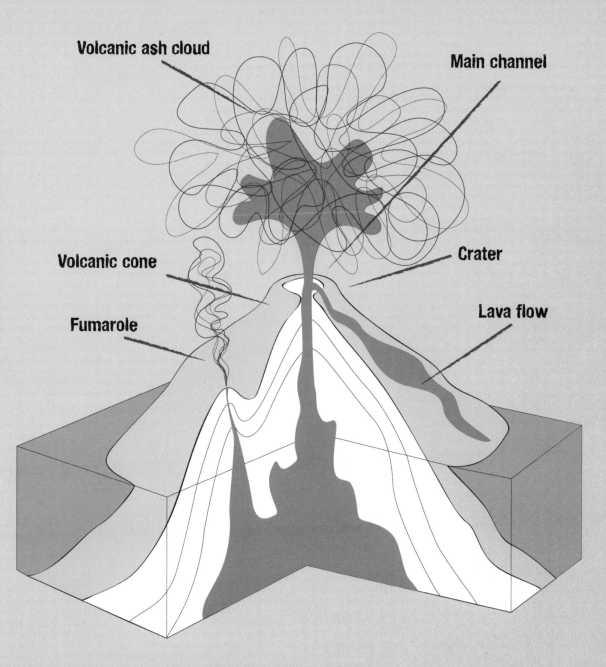

Volcanic ash cloud

Main channel

Volcanic cone

Crater

Fumarole

Lava flow

THE EXTERNAL SHAPE CAN REVEAL A LOT OF VALUABLE INFORMATION

The shape of a volcano shows you what sort of eruptions took place: whether they were quiet or explosive, and when they happened. Eruptions are very interesting phenomena. What happens when a volcano erupts? Pushing with extreme force from the depths of the earth, molten rock, known as 'magma', sometimes passes through the solid layers of the planet and reaches the surface. This creates craters or openings from which dust, gas, steam and molten minerals emerge, which later solidify.

Eruptions have been classified into different types, with two of these bearing the names of two volcanoes in the archipelago: Strombolian and Vulcanian eruptions.

Strombolian eruptions involve a small but continuous lava flow. The lava is semi-fluid, the flow lasts for quite a long time, and there are the ejection of lapilli and small but sporadic explosions every few hours or minutes.

Vulcanian eruptions involve short explosive events that can go on for a number of hours, or sometimes only a few minutes. The lava that is expelled is viscous. It contains explosive gases which cool very quickly, leading to short lava flows. These types of eruptions give rise to volcanoes with steep sides.

LAKE MALAWI

Lake Malawi is located at the entrance to a huge fault line dating back 40 million years, known as the Great Rift Valley, which runs across the Earth's crust separating two large African tectonic plates from the Arabian Plate. This lake is one of the deepest in the world and its waters are warm and clear. Many of the animals that live here aren't found anywhere else and have unique features that have developed over a very long time.

Like the Galapagos Islands, this lake in the heart of Africa has remained isolated and is a real laboratory where you can observe the surprising effects of evolutionary adaptation on plants and animals.

The park area surrounding the lake is covered by forests and wooded savannas where small fishing communities live. The first human settlements date back to the Iron Age. The shores of Lake Malawi are home to hippopotamuses, waterbuck antelopes and baboons, in addition to African fish eagles and kingfishers.

This giant baobab tree is found on the lake shore. This typical African tree may be more than 800 years old. The famous explorer David Livingstone is said to have often stopped under this tree to tell of his adventures.

Livingstone was the first European to reach the lake in 1859, after discovering the Victoria Falls a few years before.

THE GREAT RIFT VALLEY

The Great Rift Valley separates the Nubian Plate to the west from the Somali Plate and the Arabian Plate to the east. It starts in southern Africa and ends in Syria, 3,977 miles away. Today, only the southern part is recognizable as a large depression and it is where, besides Lake Malawi, other famous lakes such as Lake Tanganyika, Lake Victoria and Lake Albert are located. It then continues through Eritrea before disappearing under the Red Sea. Plate movements not only gave rise to the lakes but also to the major volcanic phenomena that led to the formation of Mount Kenya and Mount Kilimanjaro.

The cichlids of Lake Malawi

Lake Malawi and the other lakes to the north like Lake Tanganyika are famous for the incredibly diverse cichlids, a family of freshwater fish that developed in these waters in a situation of total isolation. Dozens of species unique to the region have been counted, some of which have colorings that greatly resemble those of fish living in tropical coral reefs.

In addition to their bright colors, they have a very noble appearance and elegant movements.

CICHLIDS ARE ALSO WELL-KNOWN BECAUSE ONCE THEIR EGGS HAVE BEEN FERTILIZED, THE FEMALES KEEP THEM SAFE AND WARM IN THEIR MOUTHS! EVEN AFTER HATCHING, THE FRY – THE NAME FOR VERY YOUNG FISH – STAY IN THEIR MOTHERS' MOUTHS FOR SEVERAL DAYS SO THAT THEY CAN GROW THERE SAFE FROM DANGER.

WHAT IS THEIR BIGGEST THREAT?

Besides pollution, the main threat to the survival of these fish is the introduction of fish and plants from other places into this ecosystem.

Who knows how long it will take these beautiful and colorful fish to adapt to the newcomers and whether they will survive?

Beauty with wings

The shores of the lake are home to many flamingos. These beautiful birds are pink because they feed on microorganisms rich in carotene, such as blue-green algae, green algae and small fish and crustaceans.

THE NILE CROCODILE

In spite of its name, the Nile crocodile is common to many African countries, making a home wherever there is a little water.

Despite its size – 20 feet in length and 265 lbs – it can travel long distances in the dry season just to find a pool it can plunge into.

THERE ARE MANY BIRD ENTHUSIASTS LURKING IN THE TALL GRASS, BEHIND BUSHES AND SOMETIMES IN THE LEAVES OF THE TREES, TRYING TO SEE WHAT THE BIRDS ARE DOING. THEY'RE CALLED BIRD-WATCHERS. BIRD-WATCHING IS A FANTASTIC EXPERIENCE, BUT THERE ARE RULES YOU HAVE TO FOLLOW.

The 3 rules of BIRDWATCHING

1. The safety and well-being of the birds come first!

2. Never disturb the birds, especially during mating. So you have to be quiet and careful with your movements.

3. Respect the environment and don't leave anything behind but your footprints.

A river delta

When a river flows across a plain, the speed of the current decreases and the waters begin to release the sediments they carry, resulting in the deposition of sand and clay. This is how marshes are formed. These are vast areas of almost still water interspersed with islands and channels. Marshland vegetation quickly takes root on the banks, giving rise to one of the richest and most fertile ecosystems in the planet, a favorite habitat of fish and aquatic birds.

In the Danube Delta, you can observe gray herons, great egrets and purple herons – one of the rarest species of heron in Europe. They have a long neck and a long harpoon-like beak that they use to catch fish and frogs with lightning speed.

Ferruginous duck ("Aythya nyroca")

This is a brown duck, also known as the fudge duck because of its color. The Danube Delta is one of the last few places they can be seen.

White pelican ("Pelecanus onocrotalus")

These birds are great travelers. They leave the Nile Delta and the Red Sea coast in March for the Danube Delta where they make their nests. They spend most of their time catching fish. They eat more than two pounds of fish a day!

DANUBE DELTA

The Danube Delta is the largest and best preserved river mouth in Europe. Before entering the Black Sea, the river flows over an area of flat terrain, where it is divided and transformed into a giant mosaic of small channels, stagnant waters, marshes and forests of oaks, willows and poplars.

The existence of this large and well-preserved wetland area has drawn sizeable populations of birds, particularly migratory birds. The Danube Delta lies under the main flyways and more than 300 bird species can be spotted during the spring and summer migrations.

In winter, the Delta is home to more than one million individual birds that come from the North, such as swans and wild ducks, which prefer to migrate to the milder climate of this place.

The Danube Delta is ranked third in the world for the greatest biodiversity. Close to 5,500 plant and animal species live here.

WHY DO BIRDS MOVE FROM ONE PLACE TO ANOTHER?

Migrating is mainly about food. Birds go where there is an abundance of things to eat. Whether and when a bird travels is regulated by mechanisms that haven't been fully studied yet. There are hormones and other stimuli linked to variations in temperature and daylight hours that tell them when it is time to depart.

There are still many things that are not understood about migratory systems; for example, why certain birds permit some of their species to stay 'at home' while the rest of the group migrates. One of the few things we do know is that the birds take advantage of favorable air currents. After all, when you have to travel thousands of miles, having the wind behind you is certainly an advantage. How do they know where to go? This is one of the most incredible natural instincts that scientists are still making great efforts to study.

Birds have an internal compass and something akin to a map that they follow, just as ancient mariners followed the stars and magnetic fields in order to reach their destination.

The northernmost part of Sweden is an area covered in pine forests that are interspersed with lakes, marshes and wet meadows dotted with dwarf birch trees. This land is home to the Lapps, also known as the Saami, the only humans able to live so close to the North Pole. The Saami have lived in Laponia for over 4,000 years and live in complete harmony with the animals they raise: reindeer. In order to survive and to let their animals survive, the Saami must live in harmony with the rhythm of nature; they need to have perfect knowledge of the life cycle of their animals, to know when the salmon they eat start to lay their eggs and where and to know where they can always find new pastures.

The Saami don't only live in Laponia with their reindeer: they also live in Norway, Finland and Russia, because nature knows no borders.

A CALENDAR WITH EIGHT SEASONS

In Saami culture, the concept of time is linked to the main climate events, to the seasons and to their reindeers' behavior and life cycle. The Saami follow the rules set down by nature and respect all of its markers. Everything that happens is always noted down on a small calendar that is easy to carry. The calendar has two purposes: it serves to record both the major climate changes during the year and the main religious events. The information gathered is for the entire community and future generations. The calendar used to be made from wood or reindeer antlers and the information would be written in runes.

NOT EXACTLY A MILD CLIMATE

Summers in Laponia are like in most other places or even better. The weather from June to August is very good and you can even bathe in the lakes. The sun never sets, although this makes it difficult to sleep. Then the fall begins, which is only two weeks long. From October to May life is hard because outside, where the elk live, the temperature can go from 26.6 to -22° F. The sky is always changeable and you never see the sun. Winter ends with the return of the sun, which melts all the ice and snow in less than a month.

COLORS OF THE NORTH

When you look at the sky this far north, if there aren't any clouds you can see a green beam along the horizon.
This is the aurora borealis, also known as the Northern Lights. The Earth's magnetic forces, which are normally invisible to the human eye, collide with energy from the sun – solar wind – charged with particles to produce this breathtaking effect. Sometimes this clash of forces is so strong that it causes havoc, not only with simple radios, but also with expensive satellites.

CERTAIN ANIMALS, LIKE THE ARCTIC FOX, CHANGE THE COLOR OF THEIR COAT TO AVOID BEING SEEN BY POTENTIAL ENEMIES. THE ONES THAT LIVE IN THE FAR NORTH TURN AS WHITE AS THE SNOW.

Today the great forests of the north are the habitat of some of the most amazing animals in Europe. These include brown bears, elks and the white-tailed sea eagle. Smaller but equally well-known animals include martens, arctic foxes and lemmings, small rodents native to northern meadows that reproduce at an incredible speed when they have enough food to eat.
The elk or moose is the largest herbivore in the Northern Hemisphere. It can weigh 1100 lbs and grow to a shoulder height of five feet. Males grow beautiful antlers every year. They regenerate before mating and can reach a width of six and a half feet.
The Saami have over 400 words for reindeer!

WHO SAID THAT IT NEVER GETS COLD IN AFRICA?

More importantly, who said that it never snows in Africa? The large volcanic massif of Mount Kilimanjaro, Africa's highest mountain, lies on the border of Kenya and Tanzania. The inhabitants of the region call it the 'shining mountain' or the 'white mountain', and there's a good reason for it!

This huge mountain is covered with a white cap of perennial snow. Emerging from it are the three volcano cones of Kibo (3.6 miles), Mawenzi (3.2 miles) and Shira (2.5 miles).

As you leave the icy expanses and head down towards the immense plains, you pass through the high steppes where small plants and lichen grow. They have adapted to what is more like a high-altitude desert. Between 1.9 and 2.5 miles, the outlines of large plants like lobelia and giant groundsel emerge from the rocky terrain, overcoming the challenge of an environment where life is very difficult for plants. A little lower down, everything would be so much easier for them: just under the 1.9 mile line, the mountain is covered with thick rainforest where there is abundant water and the temperatures are much higher.

LIVING AT HIGH ALTITUDE

In this environment, where the days are hot and the nights are very cold, survival for plants is difficult, but not impossible.

The giant groundsel, for instance, is prepared to deal with extreme conditions.

Its trunk can grow to a height of 33 feet and is a sort of reservoir that the plant uses to store water, which is often scarce.

Even the leaves play their part: when they are dry, they remain attached to the trunk and form a protective wrapping for the buds, shielding them from the icy nights – just like a blanket!

The first Westerner to see the snows of Mount Kilimanjaro was Johannes Rebmann, who arrived in 1848. Nobody in Europe could believe him!

How could there be snow in Africa? Now, the glacier that is found at the summit is named after him.

```
6195 m
5000 m  SUMMIT
4000 m  HIGH-ALTITUDE DESERT
2700 m  HEATH                Trees
1800 m  RAINFOREST
```

THE BEARDED VULTURE

The bearded vulture is a bird with a 6.5-foot wingspan.

It feeds on the bones of large mammals and has invented a clever method to avoid damaging its beak: it drops the bones from high in the air so that they break. Then it swallows the pieces whole, including the highly nutritious bone marrow. A minimum effort results in maximum efficiency.

KILIMANJARO NATIONAL PARK

Mount Kilimanjaro is quite young in geological terms.

It all began two million years ago when large amounts of molten rock ('magma') from below the Earth's crust poured out onto the African plain. This volcanic activity grew stronger 700,000 years ago, giving rise to three craters – Kibo, Mawenzi and Shira. So much lava came out of them that an almost 3.7-mile high mountain was created when it cooled. It took a long time, but there was finally a mountain on the equator! How long did it take? Kibo was active for 100,000 years and scientists believe it's the only crater lava could come out of again, but who knows when! There is very little volcanic activity today and erosion by wind, snow and ice has had more impact in shaping the mountain than any other process.

Elephants and giraffes prefer to stay on the plain where warm weather is guaranteed.

On clear days, you can see Kilimanjaro from a distance of 310 miles.

BRRRRRRRRR

There are so many animals in Africa and they are mostly used to a hot and dry climate. But everything is different in Kilimanjaro National Park! It's cold at the top and it rains a lot at lower altitudes.

What animals live on Mount Kilimanjaro? There are some really interesting animals high up the mountain. Small antelopes such as the bushbuck and Abbot's duiker can be found, as well as monkeys like the Western black and white colobus and the Eastern black and white colobus, which have beautiful long black and white hair – very practical for protecting it from the cold. The rainforests at the foot of the mountain are patrolled by the crowned eagle, one of the largest African eagles and a specialist at capturing monkeys and small antelopes.

Is it a huge white cloud or a cascade of ice? From a distance it isn't easy to work out what these strange white staircases are made of. Anyway, who could possibly have thought of creating something so peculiar in the middle of the Turkish countryside?

Could it have been an architect with a love for strange shapes? No. The architect in this case was water.

From deep inside the ground in this part of Turkey, there are springs of water rich in minerals, especially calcium carbonate. This is a material like chalk, the stuff you use to write on a blackboard or for drawing.

Besides being rich in calcium carbonate, the spring in Pamukkale is hot, very hot indeed. The water temperature is between 95 and 212° F. When it comes into contact with the air, part of the water evaporates, dispersing the calcium carbonate over the surrounding rocks. First it forms a thin fragile and soft layer; then it hardens, creating pools and steps of bright white limestone and travertine.

These naturally formed cascades rise to a height of 525 feet. The ancient Turks called it the 'cotton castle'.

A THOUSAND YEARS TO FORM A COLUMN

Have you ever been inside a cave? In some caves where there is water dripping, unusual sculptures can form. These sharp white spikes that decorate the ceiling and ground inside caves like marble columns are formations similar to the calcified pools and terraces of Pamukkale. They are stalactites and stalagmites, and they are formed by the constant dripping of water that is rich in calcium bicarbonate.

When it comes into contact with the air of the cave, the water releases calcium carbonate, which accumulates in a succession of layers. This increases the thickness and complexity of the rock formations. Stalactites start from the roof. One drop at a time, they grow downwards. The same drop hitting the ground produces a stalagmite, which grows upwards as the calcium carbonate is deposited over it. A column is formed when a stalactite and a stalagmite meet.

HEALING WATER

In ancient times, the Greeks and Romans discovered that water can help cure the body of certain illnesses. People only needed to immerse themselves in certain natural pools, which were like huge puddles only deeper and with cleaner water, for the health of their skin to improve. Or they could drink a few glasses of water in the morning before breakfast to clean the liver, an organ in the human body that cleans the blood, which is also cleaner as a result!

They could also breathe in the vapors to heal a cough and other problems with their respiratory systems.

For centuries, soldiers and gladiators, ordinary citizens and important figures of society spent hours immersed in natural pools of warm water. While the waters were only believed to be beneficial in those days, scientists today have discovered that the combination of mineral salts and high temperatures are in fact a natural medicine for all kinds of problems. Combined with rest in such a beautiful setting, this can be especially good for your mind!

A TEMPLE WITH SPECIAL EFFECTS

The Greeks built many temples to their gods in Hierapolis. The temple of Apollo, the god of art, medicine and music, had a special feature: it was built on a deep crack and steam came out of it.

For people entering the temple, this effect was amazing! Wrapped in a cloud of smoke, they had the feeling that they were in heaven, close to Apollo.

HIERAPOLIS, AN ANCIENT TOURIST DESTINATION

The ancient Greeks founded the city of Hierapolis in the third century BC over the calcium carbonate cascades of Pamukkale. The entire city was designed to satisfy the demands of the tourists of the time who came to immerse themselves in the thermal waters. Like today's tourists, they also wanted luxurious villas to stay in, as well as temples and theatres: everything to make a perfect holiday.

When the Romans conquered the land, they were very pleased to discover this marvel. They were also big fans of thermal baths; in fact, they had built hundreds all over their empire. Thanks to the Romans, the city continued to grow and prosper until the third century AD, because the city lay on the road to the East, and also because the Romans began to use the hot water pools to wash and dye wool.

VICTORIA FALLS

In the heart of Southern Africa, the River Zambezi flows peacefully between the hills and marshes of Zambia. At a particular point in its journey to the Indian Ocean, a huge chasm on the border with Zimbabwe forces it to make an incredible drop. The water falls 330 feet! The noise and mist from this falling mass of water can be seen from a great distance in any season, but especially in March and April, when the heavy rains make the river flood. The water then strikes the rocks with an unimaginable force.

The water entering existing cracks deepens them and gives new shapes to everything in its path. This erosion process has lasted about 10,000 years, forming new falls and gorges and making the cataracts even more spectacular.

The vegetation around the falls is lush and contrasts sharply with the savanna landscape. Billions of tiny water droplets that the waterfall sprays around it allow this unusual band of tropical vegetation to thrive in this area.

Why does this waterfall have a woman's name? The first European to come here was David Livingstone after having traveled along the River Zambezi by canoe. When he discovered the falls, he named them after the Queen of England, whose name was, of course, Victoria.

The local name for the falls is Mosi-oa-Tunya or 'smoke that thunders' because of the noise and the huge amount of spray, which looks like smoke.

A CENTURY OLD BUT NOT SHOWING ITS AGE

The bridge at Victoria Falls is a one hundred-year-old work of engineering! It was built in 1905 over the second gorge of the falls in only 14 months. It is suspended at a height of 420 feet only a short distance from the falls. The bridge is crossed by people on foot and in cars, and even by the trains connecting Zimbabwe with Zambia. Today, it's a favorite place for bungee jumpers, who come to see the falls upside down!

HOW IS A WATERFALL FORMED?

When a gently flowing river encounters a dip in its path, it has to run down it, creating a waterfall. How are these 'steps' formed? The Earth's crust, which often moves and is under pressure in several places, sometimes rises or sinks. A strong earthquake or a volcanic eruption can create steps of this kind. This is how the Victoria Falls were formed. The water of the Zambezi falls from a basalt step into a chasm in the Earth. Wherever the land and rocks leave even a little space, the water starts working to design new and amazing landscapes.

JUMPING CHAMPION

Living along the hottest and steepest gorges, like many rocky habitats in southern Africa, is a miniature antelope that is only as big as a dog — the Klipspringer. It specializes in eating the few plants that live on the almost vertical walls.

325 feet

VICTORIA FALLS IN NUMBERS

- Height: 325 feet
- Length: 5,605 feet
- Record flow: 452,028 cubic feet per second
- In the months of February and March, when the Zambezi is in flood, more than **132 million gallons** of water flows over the waterfall every minute. In less than two minutes it could fill a glass of water for every one of the Earth's inhabitants!

ANSWERS

Page 5

The Galapagos Penguins live further north than any other penguins, in moderate, not too cold water. They are endemic to the islands (meaning they are only present there).

All other penguin species live more towards the south of the Southern Hemisphere. Most penguins, like the well-known Emperor Penguin, live in Antarctica. Other species can be found in the most southern parts of South-America, in South-Africa and New Zealand.

Page 11

The "Scincus scincus", the Mulga snake and monitor lizards are reptiles.
The "Scincus scincus" is a 16 inches long lizard. They live in groups in desert tunnels and only come out to eat.
The Mulga snake is a venomous snake. He is related to the Cobra and grows to about 10 feet long.
The Monitor lizard is a predatory lizard that runs very fast.

The Wallaby is a relatively small kangaroo that lives in the forest. The Red Kangaroo is the largest species (6.6 feet tall, and he can jump up to 30 feet far). He lives in dry areas.

The Bilby and Bettong are marsupials (they have a pouch). They have long hind legs to jump with.
The Bilby looks like a rabbit and the Bettong resembles a large rat.

CREDITS

Pg 4 © Stuart Westmorland/Gettyimages, pg 6 © Karen Massier/Gettyimages, pg 9 © Theo Allofs/CORBIS, pg 10 © Nawasan. Gettyimages, pg 12 © Yann Arthus-Bertrand/CORBIS, pg 14 © Karen Su/Gettyimages, pg 17 © Theo Allofs/Gettyimages, pg 18 © Jean du Boisberranger/GettyImages, pg 20 © James Baigrie/GettyImages, pg 22 © Arthur Morris/CORBIS, pg 23 © Ed Kashi/CORBIS, pg 24 © Francesco Tomasinelli, pg 25 top © Francesco Tomasinelli, pg 25 bottom © Anders Ekholm/Gettyimages, pg 27 © DLILLC. CORBIS, pg 28 © Steve Satushek/Gettyimages, pg 30 © Francesco Tomasinelli.